MORTIMER

STORY · ROBERT MUNSCH

ART · MICHAEL MARTCHENKO

ANNICK PRESS LTD.

TORONTO • NEW YORK

Twenty-fourth printing, January 2000

Annick Press Ltd.

We acknowledge the support of the Canada Council for the Arts, the Ontario Arts
Council, and the Government of Canada through the Book Publishing Industry
Development Program (BPIDP) for our publishing activities.

Cataloguing in Publication Data
   Munsch, Robert N., 1945–
    Mortimer

   (Munsch for kids)
   ISBN 0-920303-12-9 (bound) ISBN 0-920303-11-0 (pbk.)

   I. Martchenko, Michael. II. Title. III. Series:
   Munsch, Robert N., 1945– .Munsch for kids.

PS8576.U58M67 1985 jC813'.54   C84-099722-1
PZ7.M86Mo 1985

Distributed in Canada by: Published in the U.S.A. by Annick Press (U.S.) Ltd.
Firefly Books Ltd.   Distributed in the U.S.A. by:
3680 Victoria Park Avenue   Firefly Books (U.S.) Inc.
Willowdale, ON   P.O. Box 1338
M2H 3K1   Ellicott Station
                             Buffalo, NY 14205

Printed and bound in Canada by
Friesens, Altona, Manitoba

The mother shut the door.
Then she went back down the stairs—
thump thump thump thump thump.

As soon as she got back downstairs
Mortimer sang,

Clang, clang, rattle-bing-bang
Gonna make my noise all day.
Clang, clang, rattle-bing-bang
Gonna make my noise all day.

Mortimer's father heard all that noise.
He came up the stairs—

thump thump thump thump thump thump.

He opened the door and yelled,

"MORTIMER, BE QUIET."

Mortimer shook his head, yes.

The father went back down the stairs—
thump thump thump thump thump.

As soon as he got to the bottom of the
stairs Mortimer sang,

Clang, clang, rattle-bing-bang
Gonna make my noise all day.
Clang, clang, rattle-bing-bang
Gonna make my noise all day.

All of Mortimer's seventeen brothers
and sisters heard that noise, and they
all came up the stairs—

thump thump thump thump thump thump thump.

They opened the door and yelled in a
tremendous, loud voice,

"MORTIMER, BE QUIET."

Mortimer shook his head, yes.

The brothers and sisters shut the door and went downstairs—
thump thump thump thump thump.

As soon as they got to the bottom of the stairs Mortimer sang,

Clang, clang, rattle-bing-bang
Gonna make my noise all day.
Clang, clang, rattle-bing-bang
Gonna make my noise all day.

They got so upset that they called the police. Two policemen came and they walked very slowly up the stairs—

thump thump thump thump thump thump.

They opened the door and said in very deep, policemen-type voices,

"MORTIMER, BE QUIET."

The policemen shut the door and went
back down the stairs—
thump thump thump thump thump.

As soon as they got to the bottom of the
stairs Mortimer sang,

Clang, clang, rattle-bing-bang
Gonna make my noise all day.
Clang, clang, rattle-bing-bang
Gonna make my noise all day.

Well, downstairs no one knew what to do.
The mother got into a big fight with the
policemen.
The father got into a big fight with the
brothers and sisters.

Other books in the Munsch for Kids series:

The Dark
Mud Puddle
The Paper Bag Princess
The Boy in the Drawer
Jonathan Cleaned Up, Then He Heard a Sound
Murmel Murmel Murmel
Millicent and the Wind
The Fire Station
Angela's Airplane
David's Father
Thomas' Snowsuit
50 Below Zero
I Have to Go!
Moira's Birthday
A Promise is a Promise
Pigs
Something Good
Show and Tell
Purple, Green and Yellow
Wait and See
Where is Gah-Ning?
From Far Away
Stephanie's Ponytail
Muncshworks
Munschworks 2

Many Munsch titles are available in French and/or
Spanish. Please contact your favorite supplier.